D0559751

# IT'S NOT MY FAULT I KNOW EVERYTHING

## THINK YOU CAN HANDLE JAMIE KELLY'S FIRST YEAR OF DIARIES?

#1 LET'S PRETEND THIS NEVER HAPPENED

#2 MY PANTS ARE HAUNTED!

#3 AM I THE PRINCESS OR THE FROG?

#4 NEVER DO ANYTHING, EVER

#5 CAN ADULTS BECOME HUMAN?

#6 THE PROBLEM WITH HERE IS THAT IT'S WHERE I'M FROM

#7 NEVER UNDERESTIMATE YOUR DUMBNESS

#8 IT'S NOT MY FAULT I KNOW EVERYTHING

#9 THAT'S WHAT FRIENDS <u>AREN'T</u> FOR

#10 THE WORST THINGS IN LIFE ARE ALSO FREE

#11 OKAY, SO MAYBE I DO HAVE SUPERPOWERS

#12 ME! (JUST LIKE YOU, ONLY BETTER)

## AND DON'T MISS YEAR TWO!

YEAR TWO #1: SCHOOL. HASN'T THIS GONE ON LONG ENOUGH?

YEAR TWO #2: THE SUPER-NICE ARE SUPER-ANNOYING

YEAR TWO #3: NOBODY'S PERFECT. I'M AS CLOSE AS IT GETS.

YEAR TWO #4: WHAT I DON'T KNOW MIGHT HURT ME

Jim Benton's Tales from Mackerel Middle School

# DEAR DUMB DIARY,

## IT'S NOT MY FAULT I KNOW EVERYTHING

SCHOLASTIC INC.

ISBN 978-0-439-82597-9



21 20 19 18 17 16 13 14 15 16/0
Printed in the U.S.A. 40
First printing, March 2009

*For all the Jamies, Angelines, and Isabellas of the world; I hope you don't mind me using your name.*

*Special thanks to the team at Scholastic: Steve Scott, Cheryl Weisman, Susan Jeffers Casel, Anna Bloom, and most of all, editor Shannon Penney.*

*And thanks to Mary K for all your help.*

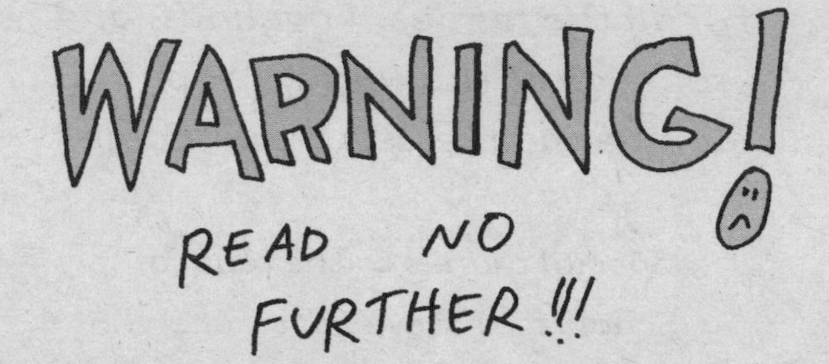
WARNING!
READ NO FURTHER!!!

DO NOT VIOLATE THE SACRED SECRECY OF THIS DIARY!

EVERYBODY KNOWS THAT

**SACRED SECRECY**

IS THE MOST

**SECRETEST**

KIND OF ALL!!!

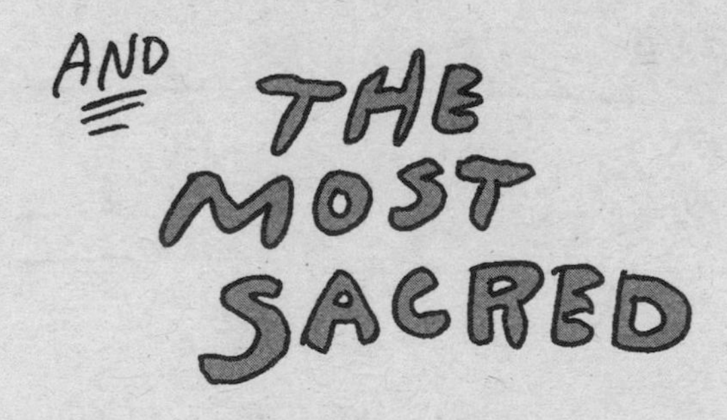


SO STOP READING MY DIARY!!!

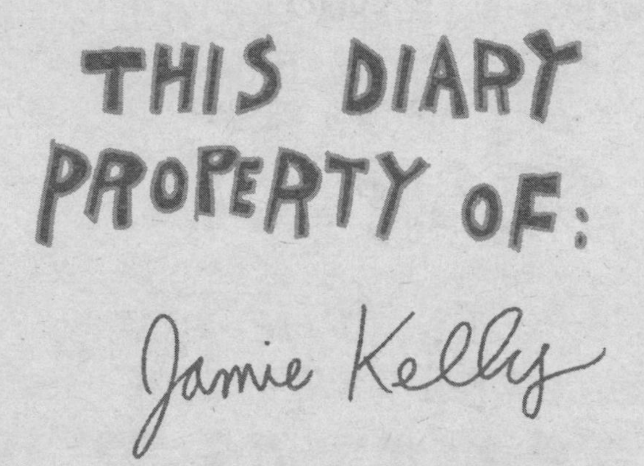


SCHOOL: Mackerel Middle School

Occupation: GENIUS

BEST FRIEND: ISABELLA

UNBEST FRIEND: ANGELINE

BOYS WHO LIKE ME: maybe all of them But for sure HUDSON

Dear Whoever Is Reading My Dumb Diary,

Are you sure you're supposed to be reading somebody else's diary? I mean, you must know about the **SACRED SECRECY OF THE DIARY** — it's a principle that must never be violated. Unless you were to find yourself in a position where you **HAD** to read another person's diary. Like if a bear or teacher or animal like that **MADE** you do it, then you wouldn't have a choice. Or if you just really really really really needed to know something, and there were at least four or more "reallys" involved, then that might be okay. And if there were some sort of zombie-related issues.

But none of these conditions apply to parents, so if you are my parents, then you are just committing unauthorized reading, and if you punish me for anything I may have written here, then I will cleverly know that you read my diary, which you do **not** have my permission to do. (Although I might be able to overlook it in exchange for a puppy.)

Now, by the power vested in me, I do promise that everything in this diary is true, or, at least, as true as I think it needs to be.

Signed,

Jamie Kelly

**PS:** Also if you are a blond girl at my school whose initials are Angeline the Blondwad, you aren't allowed to read my diary, either. Even if zombies are about to eat you.

**PPS:** Especially if they are.

## Sunday 01

Dear Dumb Diary,

It's not my fault I know everything.

Okay, I don't know where Timbuktu is, but I **refuse** to know that. Even if somebody told me, I would flush my brain like a Thought-Potty and wave good-bye to Timbuktu as it swirled down my brain hole.

I know everything that I *want* to know.

Good bye TIMBUKTU!
Goodbye OLD GUYS from OLD HISTORY!
GOOD BYE to that one KIND of MATH EVERYBODY HATES!

Sunday is the day that many of the world's great civilizations set aside to do homework. Isabella came over today so we could do homework together, which makes the time we waste **not** doing it go faster.

To mask the scent of homework, she brought over a bunch of magazines with quizzes and pictures of celebrities. We noticed how ugly people turn nice-looking by being famous — like there's this one boy on this one TV show, and if he wasn't on a TV show he would look like a girl that had been bitten horribly on the face by an ape, but since he's on TV, he looks like a girl that was bitten handsomely on the face by an angel.

Remember how I know everything? The reason this came up today is that these magazines feature lots of important quizzes and tests you can take, like ARE YOU A FASHION HIT OR FASHION TWIT? and JUST HOW MUCH NICENESS DO YOU HAVE? and ARE YOUR PARENTS ANNOYING OR SUPER-ANNOYING?

Magazine people are Geniuses and supercool because they can figure out your whole life with multiple-choice questions. I think they should make it so all Life's Questions are multiple choice.

WHEN I GROW UP I WANT TO BE:
A) A BIG BRAINLESS NINNY
B) A MEAN AND SOUR OLD TURD
C) A RICH, HAPPY ROCK STAR

Isabella kept getting mad at me because I always came out in the very top of the ratings in these quizzes. She kept coming out a little bit subhuman and said that we need better magazines with better tests. Then she tore them into a jillion pieces.

As I tried to put some of the pictures back together, I realized that the famous boy-girl actually looked better with most of his face torn off than he did when he was just famous.

Other Ways Famous-But-Uglies can improve their LOOKS.
HIRE UGLIER PEOPLE TO STAND CLOSE TO MAKE THEM SEEM LESS UGLY BY COMPARISON.

LOOK IT ME

TRY TO BECOME EVEN FAMOUSER.

TAPE THEIR PAYCHECK TO THEIR FACE.

# Monday 02

Dear Dumb Diary,

I went back and read some of my very oldest diaries. There were no entries about **important matters** like Hudson Rivers — eighth cutest boy in my grade — or things that should happen to Angeline.

The entries say things like "I eated salad dressing" and "I got a Barbie shoe stuck in Stinker's nose again" and "The vet was mean to me about the Barbie shoe so I tried to bite him but vets are quick at not getting bit because dogs try all the time but dogs don't usually kick so I did that."

What amazed me was just how **dumb** I used to be, considering how smart I am now. There must have been a day when I just woke up smart.

I wish it happened to everyone.

I wonder if there was a day when Angeline woke up annoying. Like one night, she goes to bed and she's hardly perfect at all, and the next morning, she wakes up in a puddle of her own beauty, and she glides over to the mirror and radiates **gorgeous glamour** all over the place. She sees that she's the most beautiful person that has ever lived, and she smiles prettily because she knows how much it's going to **bug** me.

HAIR REMAINS NEATLY COMBED THROUGHOUT THE NIGHT
PJS REMAIN UNWRINKLED
ROOM DECOR FAR TOO CURLY-CUED

And maybe there was a moment when Hudson Rivers was only the **ninth** cutest boy in my grade, and then he cutely said some sort of cute thing and realized that now he was number **eight**????

I sort of doubt this one, because I don't think boys realize things.

## WHAT BOYS DON'T REALIZE

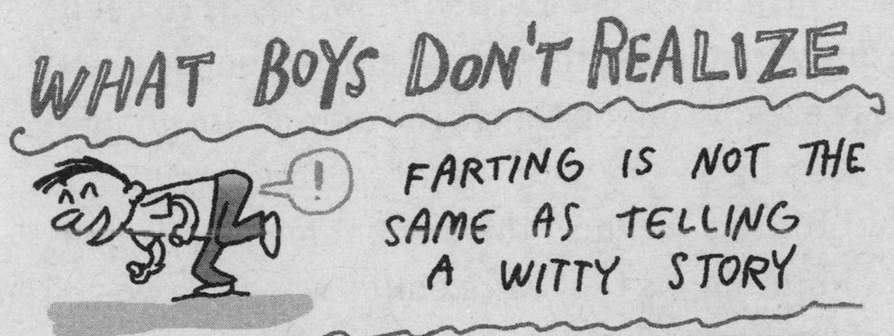

!
FARTING IS NOT THE SAME AS TELLING A WITTY STORY


IN ANCIENT TIMES, THERE WERE NO VIDEO GAMES AND ANCIENT BOYS DID OTHER THINGS FOR FUN.

BATHING WON'T KILL YOU.

# Tuesday 03

Dear Dumb Diary,

Today, Mr. Evans gave us a new assignment in English class. **Get this:** He wants us to keep a diary for almost three weeks. This sounds pretty easy except for one thing: The diaries are going to be read by **everyone**. In fact, Evans explained that Old Mrs. Penney, the ancient media specialist (or librarian, as they were called when she was hired and books were just being invented) is going to type up all of our diary entries and put them in the library where anybody can just walk in and check them out. This is a clear violation of the **Sacred Secrecy of Diaries.**

Now, I'm an expert on diaries, as you know. That makes me a ***diareer***. Or maybe that makes me ***diaretic***. Anyway, this expertness made me blurt out, "You can't let people read our diaries. Diaries are private."

This probably would have made the point just fine, but my expertness made me add, "You've got to be out of your mind."

Experts always talk too MUCH except MAYBE EXPERTS ON SHUTTING UP which I'm NOT.

Mr. Evans's vein instantly swelled up and throbbed on his bald head like a skinny blue snake attacking a giant egg.

Isabella, who is an expert on knowing when somebody has been **Pushed Too Far**, sensed that Mr. Evans was going to punish me. She quickly blurted out, "Jamie, if you know so much about diaries, maybe you should have to help Old Mrs. Penney with the project."

Normally, I would have been mad that she had offered me up that way, but she probably spared me from something much worse. What would I do without her?

Suddenly, Mr. Evans's face looked like a big wad of cheese with a little curved cut in it, which is how his face makes a smile. He said that the diaries would be anonymous, and that was why Mrs. Penney would be typing them up — so nobody could recognize anyone's handwriting. And as far as privacy, he wanted us to understand that anything we write **MUST BE TRUE**. But since everyone could read these things, we might want to use fake names if something is very personal.

Then he said he thought that Isabella had a great idea, and even though Mrs. Penney has been doing this for decades (in fact, she even invented the assignment), she would certainly love the help of an expert like me.

**Note to Mr. Evans:** Yes, I understand sarcasm when I hear it, you pleasant, not fat, unbald, young teacher, you.

SARCASTIC DRAWING OF MR. EVANS, WHO IS SARCASTICALLY NOT MAKING ME SICK WITH HIS HEAD VEIN, WHICH I HAVE SARCASTICALLY NOT DRAWN

# Wednesday 04

Dear Dumb Diary,

Okay, so here's the deal, Dumb Diary. I have to write diary entries to hand in for my assignment, but I'm not going to stop my important regular diary work, such as documenting the number of times Hudson has sat with me and Isabella at lunch in the last month (eleven times), or the number of times he's stopped and talked to us at our lockers (eight times) or the number of times he's spit out his gum on the sidewalk this week (four times . . . why am I counting this?).

Anyway, I'll keep up my real diary as well as the fake pages, and at the end of the three weeks, I'll just tear out the Fake Diary assignment pages and turn those in.

Don't get jealous, Dumb Diary. I'm not cheating on you with this fake diary. So don't put on the saddest music you can find and write weepy poems about your broken heart or spine or whatever. It's true that I would be worth a whole bunch of VERY weepy poems, but not over this.

To be sure that I don't tear out the wrong pages and turn those in, my assignment pages will look different, and will be ***exactly*** what I'm willing to let people read.

Here's what I'm thinking my fake entries should look like:

*My Dearest Diary:*

*Today I went to school and appreciated the crap out of my teachers, especially Mr. Evans, who gave us this really awesome assignment of diary-writing that I get to do instead of watching TV.*

*Fondly,*
*Anonymous*

(NOTE HOW I'M USING A BIG THICK PEN IN MY LEFT HAND TO MAKE THE DRAWINGS IN MY FAKE DIARY LOOK DIFFERENT)

Perfect, right? Sometimes it amazes me how ingenious I am about everything.

Oh, and I stopped by the library to ask Old Mrs. Penney how she wanted me to help her and she said, "You're the one that likes to write, aren't you? And draw? Friends with Isabella?"

What was next? The color of my underpants? Evidently, Old Mrs. Penney is one of those teachers that knows **everything** about every kid in the school.

She said that once she gets the diaries from Mr. Evans, she'll explain what I have to do. Then she said something old and I didn't understand her.

*Things OLD FOLKS say that can't be fully understood by people.*

PERSNICKITY

DANGBURNED

CONSTIPATED

# Thursday 05

*My Dearest Diary:*

*Thursday, as you may have heard, is Meat Loaf Day in the cafeteria. It feels so good to know that our cooks are doing their part to make sure that the elbow meat of weasels — which is too often wastefully discarded after weasels are run over — is carefully made into lunch for me and my fellow innocent children. At least I think it is weasel elbow meat.*

*Signed,*
*Anonymous but really pretty*

Dear Dumb Diary,

Now for the real entry: Angeline has been sitting down right next to me in the cafeteria more often lately, and I think it's because she thinks we're family. Not because her uncle, Assistant Principal Devon, married my Aunt Carol (my mom's sister). No — because my dog, Stinker, and her dog, Stickybuns, had puppies together, which makes them married in **Dog World**.

DOG WEDDINGS ARE PROBABLY LIKE PEOPLE WEDDINGS except the BRIDE HAS to throw the BOUQUET 50 TIMES Because it keeps getting fetched back.

But this really doesn't make me and Angeline related, exactly. What this makes us is **Dog-in-Laws.** And in-laws — any kind of in-laws — are only family when they're around.

In-laws are like a side order that you didn't ask for that comes on the plate with the food you **did** order. And sometimes the side order you get is onion rings or grapes or something good like that, but you could also get a little cup of soggy coleslaw or deep-fried fingernails.

It's like the waiter brought the puppies over with a side order of Angeline-slaw in a giant pink bowl, and he accidentally gave me a diet drink with no ice in it. Also my fork has a hair on it and all they have for dessert is unflavored Jell-O.

Wait. Why am I writing about food? Oh, yeah. Thursday is Meat Loaf Day so I didn't eat lunch.

You remember that Isabella is getting one of the puppies right, Dumb Diary? She keeps asking if her puppy is done yet, which I don't like talking about because even though I've asked my mom over and over, she won't let me have one.

Isabella is really anxious to get a puppy because she has had six kittens run away from home, plus one turtle who is currently in the process of running away from home but only manages to get about a foot a week. He's been running away for as long as I can remember. This is giving Isabella lots of time to try to talk him out of it, but he hasn't slowed down a bit. (At least we don't **think** he has.)

I explained that it takes six or seven weeks before the puppies are ready to stop nursing and leave their mom, so her puppy can't go anywhere until sometime around the end of the month.

Isabella said that you could milk a dog like a cow and put that milk in little bottles so that the puppy could leave the mom early, and that she knew this one girl who did it to a cat and even tasted it.

When Isabella tells you something like this, you have two choices. You can tell her that she's wrong and accept the consequences, like getting yelled at, or waking up in the hospital, or having her blurt out some stupid secret thing you did once. (In my defense, I bet a lot of people have made snowmen of their secret crushes and then kissed them and had to go to the emergency room because they poked themselves in the eye with a frozen carrot.)

Or you can just nod and move on.

Secrets Only Isabella Knows
I'M AFRAID MY DEEP KOALA LOVE might make me accidentally marry somebody that looks like one.
I believe that ZOMBIES CAN NOT ATTACK IF YOU ARE UNDER THE COVERS.
For many years I believed that HAM came from HAMSTERS.

# Friday 06

*My Dearest Diary:*

*My dear friend, who I really admire for her lovely mop of blond hair and gracefully lashed eyeballs, asked me to name puppies with her after school today. I accepted, and had a gracefully lovely time.*

*Signed,*
*Anonymous and good at making odors sound feminine*

CUTENESS

DUMBNESS

Dear Dumb Diary,

What really happened: Angeline asked me to come over to her house. Since her dog, Stickybuns, and my **doglike pet**, Stinker, are the parents, she thought that we should get to name the puppies. She explained that she's no good at coming up with names, so she needed my help.

Normally, I would never consider accepting an invitation to Angeline's house out of concern that she could be there, but puppies can make people do crazy things, so I went.

A puppy's gaze can actually make a human girl melt with PURE LOVE

Angeline's family room looks a little like mine, which is pretty good evidence that she copied it off me. Her artificially cute dog, Stickybuns, was curled up in a little basket bed with the puppies that are old enough now to wriggle in and out of the basket and sniff around a little. They are still kind of **wobbly** and **clumsy** and reminded me of tiny fat naked grandpas that had taken too much of their medicine.

But I had to admit, it was all very beautiful and peaceful and kind of a miracle. It made me want one more than ever, but my mom totally went berserk last time I asked.

And then I stepped on a puppy's head.

Actually, I just *thought* that I had. There was a little stuffed chew toy on the floor and when I stepped on it, my foot thought it felt exactly like I was smushing a puppyhead. I screamed real loud, which freaked out Angeline's dog a little and sent a few puppies tumbling out of the basket, where I almost really stepped on one because I was sort of hopping around trying not to.

This made Stickybuns get all nervous and it made Angeline laugh harder than I had ever heard her laugh. For just a second, it sounded almost human, and I actually started laughing myself.

I believe that this is purely the result of inhaling concentrated puppy fumes, which can make people laugh and create "**awwww**" sounds against their will. It's not like Angeline and I have anything in common now.

Angeline's laughter sounds like a person's

And Angeline was right about her naming ability. She kept coming up with boring names like Sue and Joe. I came up with excellent names, so I wound up naming all four puppies.

Considering what a grossface their dad is, three of them are pretty adorable. I named them **Prince Fuzzybutt**, **Dingledongle**, and **The Bubblegum Duchess**. Tragically, one of the puppies looks just like Stinker, so I named her **Stinkette**. Although this name is based on an odor, I made it pretty-sounding because, after all, she is a woman dog and if you are an ugly woman, hopefully you can at least have a name that is kind of pretty.

And then, Dumb Diary, **IT HAPPENED.** We were just sitting there smiling at the puppies, and Angeline ***touched my hair.***

I'm used to Isabella touching my hair. When we were younger, she touched it because you have to touch it in order to pull it. These days, Isabella touches it and says encouraging BFF things like, "Is this really hair? At some point isn't this called fur, or something? Maybe a pelt?"

But Angeline was still full of puppy fumes and laughter and she said, "I can fix this, you know. You should let me fix your hair sometime."

This is like Albert Einstein offering to help you cheat on your science test. Or like Angeline offering to help Albert Einstein with his hair.

I learned long ago that Angeline's hair looks the way it does because she **MAKES** it look that way. She wasn't born with it. I've seen pictures — her hair used to be worse than mine. For real.

"Yeah, okay," I lied, since this is way more than **JUST OKAY**. But I can't let Angeline know how important it is. She came very close to sharing some hair secrets with me once before, and it fell through. I'm positive that Angeline doesn't like me very much, so I have to be careful, like when you want to ask your parents to do something that you know they hate. Fortunately, my parents hate many things, so I have quite a bit of experience in this area.

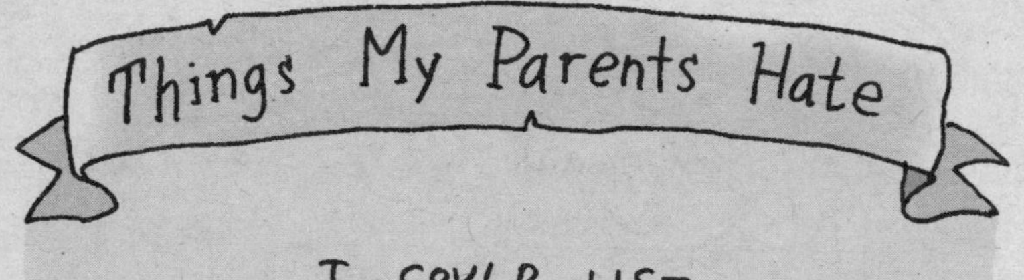


I COULD LIST THEM ALL BUT IT'S SIMPLER TO JUST LIST THE THINGS THEY DO LIKE:

LOW-PRICED GASOLINE

NAPS

TERRIBLE, TERRIBLE MUSIC.

## Saturday 07

*My Dearest Diary:*

*My best friend (who does not wear glasses or have a round head) called today and did an impression for me on the phone. Also I did a lot of really kind things for charities and was very nice to a baby.*

*Signed,*
*Anonymous and truthful*

Dear Dumb Diary,

The REAL entry: This morning Isabella called, and I knew I shouldn't tell her that I went over and named the puppies yesterday.

"I went over and named the puppies yesterday," I accidentally bragged.

Isabella got really quiet. It's hard to explain why, but quietness is actually the scariest sound Isabella makes.

AND I COULD TELL
SHE WAS LIGHTING HERSELF
IN A SCARY WAY.

Isabella asked what I named them, so I told her in this really cute voice that was so cute it made Stinker pee a little. And in spite of this strong endorsement by their father, Isabella said she didn't like any of those names and that she'll be renaming her puppy once it comes home with her. She's planning on calling it either Sugarberry or Deathbite. I told her that you can't rename a puppy. Once it has been given a name, that's what you have to call it from that moment on. This is Puppylaw, and everyone knows it.

Isabella said that you can rename anything, and that her dad got a new assistant at work and renamed him Matt because he just liked it better than saying, "Oh, Melvin, could you come in here for a moment and bring the important papers, Melvin?"

Then to prove it, she went and got her dad and put him on the phone. He said the same thing, but I'm almost positive that it was Isabella pretending to be her dad.

I was going to tell Isabella about Angeline and my hair, but it wasn't the right time. She wouldn't stop pretending that she was her dad and was threatening to ground me because, according to her/him, the law states that a dad can legally ground his child's best friend. She wouldn't stop pretending and I really didn't want to share the news with Isabella-pretending-to-be-her-dad.

And about the truthfulness of today's fake diary entry: Maybe it wasn't exactly a baby that I was nice to, maybe it was a beagle. And maybe I wasn't nice exactly. Maybe I was just **not that mean.** Anyway, I meant that I sat cowboy-style on Stinker but got up pretty quick. (Much of this is Stinker's fault. Things like this wouldn't happen if he had the decency to be cuter.)

I really think he's ugly on purpose

And I didn't do anything **against** charities today. So that's a lot like doing something for them, right? Ask any charity — they'll tell you that they appreciate it when people don't do things against them.

# Sunday 08

Dear Dumb Diary,

Isabella came over today (homework day) and brought a few more magazines so she and I could do more of their brilliant quizzes. Here's a sample question from a quiz called: ARE YOU POLITE?

If a friend bought you a really ugly shirt, would you:

A. choke her with it.

B. pretend to like it, then sell it on eBay.

C. tell her you really appreciate the gesture, but think the two of you could exchange it for one you'd wear more often.

D. get teased every time you wear it, and one day tell a psychologist that your friend is to blame for all your problems.

Isabella was just amazed to learn that the answer was "C." She wouldn't tell me what she thought the answer was, although she did say it wasn't choking because that would only make sense if it had been an ugly belt.

I did a couple more quizzes and even if I don't get every single question right, I always score in the highest bracket. It's nothing for Isabella to get all frustrated about. I'm a **Magazine Quiz Genius**, so it just naturally follows that I am a genius at everything. I mean, we have to admit: The people who write these quizzes are the brightest people in the nation. I'm sure many of them are busy saving the world with quizzes on critically important things like diseases and ecology. It's impossible to not respect findings that are so clearly correct about me.

After that, the rest of our homework went badly, and by that I mean we did our homework.

Stand by for fake entry.

*My Dearest Diary:*

*My friend and I discussed the right thing to do when receiving a gift that is not to your liking. Speaking as a proven genius, my conclusion: Never give somebody anything long enough to go around your neck.*

*Sincerely,*
*Anonymous and planning to keep breathing*

# Monday 09

Dear Dumb Diary,

Isabella whipped out a bunch of new magazines at lunch today and wanted me to do the quizzes. I was just preparing to astonish Isabella with my geniusness when Angeline sat down next to us.

Isabella explained to her that I'm a **Magazine Quiz Genius** and Angeline smiled and said, "Me, too."

There was nothing that Isabella would have rather heard, except maybe for the sound of her mean older brothers not being able to find any of their clothes on the first day of school. (It's a long story, but they had it coming to them, nobody could ever prove it was Isabella, and they had to go to school wearing their dad's big fat guy clothes.)

Isabella was delighted to hear Angeline's cheery little "Me, too" because she is very competitive. If you say you can run fast, Isabella will take off running and challenge you to keep up. If you say you have a gross toe, Isabella will take off a shoe and try to deform one of her toes to be grosser.

She's so competitive that she even likes to see competition between others — in this case, Angeline and me.

one time she wouldn't close her mouth until I admitted her tongue WAS the WORLD'S GROSSEST.
she was right.
IT IS.

Isabella flipped right to one quiz in particular called SO YOU THINK YOU KNOW EVERYTHING and began asking us the questions. We wrote the answers down secretly, so Angeline couldn't copy off me.

The first few were multiple-choice questions, and they were pretty easy to answer. Easy for me because I knew the answers, and easy for Angeline because she didn't. (It's a known Science Fact that people are wrong as fast as they are right.)

We were both humming along until Isabella came to the next question.

Angeline SNEAKILY pretending not to copy off of me, which only proves just how sneaky she is.

Isabella said, "What do people really think about you?" and she leaned back in her chair a little and smiled. There was something about how she smiled that looked like she had just thrown a stick of dynamite into a truck full of dynamite that was in a warehouse that had been built out of dynamite and the people who worked there had eaten dynamite for breakfast. (I know how this smile looks, because this is how Isabella looks whenever she thinks about something explodey.)

I know **exactly** how people feel about me. For starters, Angeline doesn't like me, Isabella does — in her own way — and Hudson has a little crush on me, but also kind of on Angeline.

Angeline looked a little confused. Probably because she's so perfectly excellent and popular, the question of how people feel about her just never comes up in her perfectly excellent and popular head. Of COURSE she knows how they feel: They Worship Her. The mere ***existence*** of such a question probably confused her.

I wish her eyes really did this

Even though I knew the answer (I know all the answers, Dumb Diary), I didn't want to say that in front of Angeline or Isabella. So I did what all famous intelligent people in history have done when they didn't want to answer a question.

I went to the bathroom. I didn't even wait to hear if there were multiple choice answers. I just said **CODE YELLOW** and bolted.

Not like Isabella would hesitate to follow me. One time when I had the flu, she came to my house and hung out in the bathroom with me because I had promised to paint her toenails. She said that I might as well paint them because I was on the floor anyway. You see, it's because of her mean older brothers that she is immune to all manners of toilet nastiness. It's really sort of a gift, like playing the violin. Or dancing. Or playing the violin and dancing while Isabella's brothers fart at you.

The **real** reason my escape worked was because I left my juice box on my tray, and you may always count on Isabella to steal your juice box when you go to the can. It's kind of amazing to see her victimize one. She holds that little straw in her teeth, and in one plunge, she can pierce the box and drain it like a mutant radioactive mosquitowoman. I've even seen her yank the straw out, and then use it to swiftly vampire the cream from the middle of a Twinkie.

And now, stay tuned for today's fake diary entry:

*My Dearest Diary:*

*Since I am a genius, I went to the bathroom. I solved my problems with juice, and I no longer challenge friends to gross toe contests.*

*Sincerely,*
*Anonymous and unable to dance while being farted upon*

# Tuesday 10

Dear Dumb Diary,

Mr. Evans wanted us to talk about the diaries today in class. But, of course, nobody really wanted to talk about them, because talking about homework is like doing it twice. And now I'm writing about not talking about it, so now it's like I'm doing it three times. I wonder if doing my homework three times like this is part of why I'm such a genius.

Isabella did not forget that I had blown off her quiz yesterday. Isabella has an excellent memory and remembers almost everything.

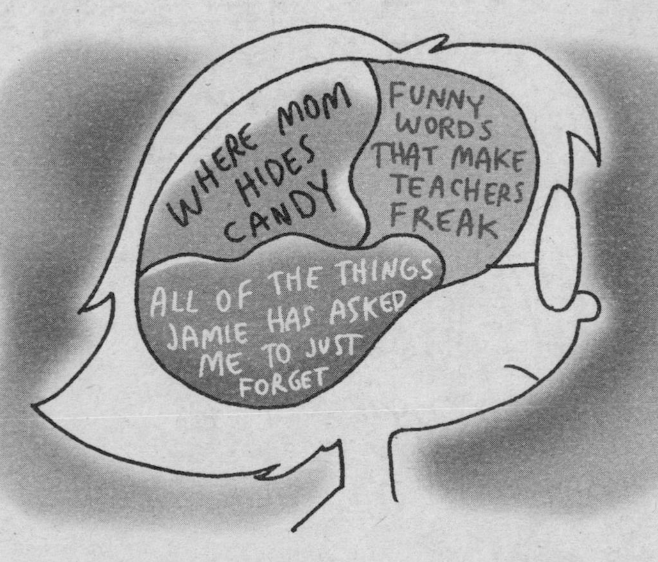

In English class, she waved the magazine quiz at me in as threatening a manner as a quiz can be waved. Mr. Evans saw Isabella shaking it at me, and me trying to tell her to put it away with just my facial expressions, and of course he just **HAD** to say something. Teachers are very nosy about things you do while they are teaching.

"Jamie," he baldly began, "is there something that you and Isabella want to say before I give you both detention?"

I had to think fast.

"Mr. Evans," I prettily answered, "I have a question about magazine quizzes."

HEY BALD GUYS:
SERIOUSLY, WATCH THE GLARE

I braced myself to look at his face and the throbbing veins within, and it didn't really look angry.

If anything, it looked a little *confused.* It wasn't the confused look he sometimes has, like when Isabella asks him language questions. Like a few weeks ago, when she asked him who makes up swear words and is that something that anybody can get a job doing because she has some good ideas for new ones.

It was more of a stunned kind of confused, like the look on somebody's face when you walk in on her and her ointment when she thought the bathroom door was locked.

"What's the question?" Mr. Evans asked, his voice squeaking a bit.

"Have you ever seen those quizzes?" I asked.

"Yes, I've seen them."

"Well, do you think it would be a good idea to answer some of the questions from those things in our diary entries? I mean, it seems like they are supersmart and might be a good place to get ideas for things to write about," I said.

Isabella kind of deflated, because she is an expert on knowing how adults and apes will react to things. And she could see how this was going to go down.

ISABELLA CAN SENSE RAGE IN GORILLAS AND TEACHERS

Mr. Evans stood up and smiled, which made me swallow my gum.

"That's a great idea, Jamie," he said. "And I think you're right: Those quizzes do have really good questions."

Later on, I explained to Isabella that **now** I'm saving my quiz answer for homework because it's easier to do that than to think up something new, and besides, it was her fault that I had to cleverly ask Evans the question in the first place. Isabella didn't like it, but working less on homework is so deeply rooted in her soul that she was unable to argue about it.

Oh, hang on. I almost forgot my fake entry.

Drawing with your wrong hand is so difficult we should have a special charity for it.

*My Dearest Diary:*

*My friend says she started pooping gum at eight years old because she's more mature than most girls her age, but that might just be bragging.*

*You see, scary teachers can be even scarier when they are unexpectedly unscary, and this can make you swallow your gum. According to my friend, Science says most people don't start pooping gum until they are at least nine years old because it takes seven years to pass through your system, and most parents don't give gum to anybody under two years old.*

*Sincerely,*
*Anonymous and I'll have to get back to you about the gum*

# Wednesday 11

Dear Dumb Diary,

Isabella asked me to take a look at a few of her diary entries for Mr. Evans's class. Diareering — or would it be "diarating"? — anyway, the keeping of a diary is one of the few areas where Isabella will admit that I am better than she is.

Here I am in my DIARARIUM, committing DIARATION in MY DIARY.

She said that she thought using ideas from magazines was a good way to make the project easier. So this was one of her entries:

Dear Diary,

I saw a phone in this magazine and I want it.

There were these shoes I saw in a magazine and I want to get them.

I want to have a car like the one I saw in this magazine.

I want to find out who invented those cards that they put in magazines because I want to stuff a dozen of them down his throat.

I want an iPod. I saw one in a magazine.

Your owner and master,
Isabella

P.S. I want more magazines.

I chose this entry because it was one of the entries that used the word "want" the least. There was one that used it less, but it used the word "demand" a lot, and it didn't really reflect Isabella's best qualities. Best *quality*. Whatever.

I told her I really liked how she described the way she felt about Magazine-Card Guy, throatwise. And I reminded her NOT to use her real name because they're going to put these in the library for anybody to read. Including Magazine-Card Guy, whoever he is.

She said she didn't care because she wants people to know how she feels about them.

And then Isabella asked to see that entry about how I think people feel about me. You know, *that question* I never got around to answering because I just don't feel like it.

To be fair, she **HAD** shown me one of her entries, and she **IS** my best friend and everything, so I figured I should do the right thing and distract her by telling her that her puppy would be ready tomorrow.

Amazing How cute a total LIE CAN Be.

Okay, maybe that was not totally completely 100 percent true. But at least it should have been true.

And when you think about it, **SHOULD HAVE BEEN TRUE BUT ISN'T** is **wayway** better than **SHOULD NOT BE TRUE BUT IS.** Also I think **wayway** should be a word, as in the sentence: Isabella was so **wayway** excited that she totally forgot about proving to me that I am not a magazine genius.

Tomorrow I'm going to have to talk to Angeline and see if I can make her understand that this is her fault, or the fault of her dog for not getting these puppies ready in time for my lie to be true. Maybe they can let one go early. Otherwise, I am going to be **wayway** in trouble with Isabella.

Oh, I almost forgot the fake diary entry. Here goes:

*My Dearest Diary:*

*Lies are something that people should not make you tell, because there is a chance that somebody could actually blame you for a lie that others put into your mouth.*

*This makes them Doubly Responsible: once for making you lie, and again for getting you blamed for it. Honestly, I don't know how some people live with themselves.*

*Sincerely,*
*Wayway Anonymous*

GOOD PERSON
FORCED
TO LIE

# Thursday 12

Dear Dumb Diary,

I managed to find Angeline before school started. It's not hard, really. You just look around for an emanation of golden light beaming up from a crowd of normal people, and in the center you will find Angeline, emanating all over everybody.

I explained to her that I didn't know how, but Isabella may have gotten the impression that her puppy might be ready to go home with her, and did Angeline think maybe we could just hurry things up a bit? I said that maybe some puppies are ready to leave home earlier than others. Like my grandpa, who always tells me how he left home when he was only seventeen and headed out into the world to seek his fame and fortune. And how kids today are no good and he needs an operation to get a new skeleton or something.

And CANDY was so cheap that when you bought some, they paid you.

Angeline said she doubted the puppies were ready to be separated from their mother. But then she said I should come over after school tomorrow and we'll have a look at them. And while I'm there, SHE'LL TRY TO DO SOMETHING WITH MY HAIR.

Even my HAIR freaked OUT

It was just like if you spotted a unicorn in your yard and didn't want to scare it away, so you lured it closer by offering it raspberry milk shakes and sequins or whatever it is unicorns eat.

"Sure, okay," I said, doing my best not to commit sudden, violent pee. "Let's not talk to Isabella about this little puppy review, though — let's make it a surprise."

Of course I knew that she'd find out sooner or later. Now that I think about it, adults are always saying that. "I'll have to do something sooner or later." Why would anybody ever pick sooner?

*"Sooner or later, you're going to break your neck if you keep that up."*

"Okay. I think that later is going to work better for me, then."

WHO WOULD PICK SOONER?
SURE GLAD I GOT THAT DONE AHEAD OF SCHEDULE.

I saw Isabella at lunch and told her that I had to check with Angeline about how we could get her the puppy. Even though my dog, Stinker, was their father, Angeline's dog was their mother, which made Angeline a mother-in-law, and you do not want to get one of *those* bent out of shape.

This was enough to make Isabella wait a little longer, since dads fear almost nothing on earth except their mothers-in-law.

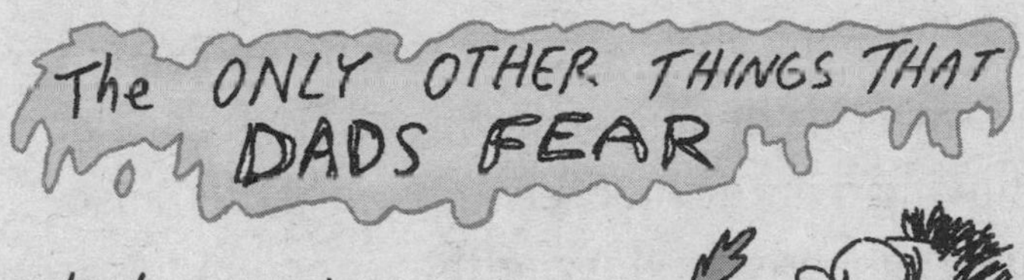
The ONLY OTHER THINGS THAT
DADS FEAR

That one day OUR PLANET WILL RUN OUT OF MEAT!!

That A LAW COULD Be PASSED REQUIRING them to wear TUXEDOS ALL the time.

THAT ONE DAY THE TV REMOTE WILL Be MISSING BRIEFLY.

# FRIDAY 13

Dear Dumb Diary,

Ohmygoshabunchofstuffhappenedtodaybutl can'treallyrememberanyofitbecauselwentoverto Angeline'shouseandshefixedmyhair. Idon'tknowwhy shedidbutshedidandnowit'sbeautiful.

Wait a second. Wait a second. I have to breathe. Oh my gosh when I breathe my nose is filled with this delicious shampoo fragrance and I'm having a hardtimebreathingnormallyI'mso excitedStinkerisbarkingandIhavetocalmdownfora minutebeforelwriteanymoreIfeelalittledizzy.

OMG
I CAN HARDLY
DRAW I CAN
HARDLY DRAW

Okay. I'm okay now. I laid down for a while and Stinker finally stopped barking at me. But I think I know why he was barking — he hardly even recognized me with My Gorgeous New Hair. I look like an entirely different person. Also, I think I might have been standing on his foot.

So, I went over to Angeline's house earlier and we talked about the puppies. Whatever, blah blah blah.

The main thing of all MAIN THINGS is that ANGELINE FIXED MY HAIR. She did a little shampooing, some conditioning, combing, trimming, a spritz of this and a spray of that, and now my hair looks exactly like hers, except for instead of being golden-blond, mine is this shimmering-toasted-auburn-brunette color that is the exact same color as the most delicious things on earth's menus.

My head looks like this ridiculously expensive teddy bear that first you fall in love with, and then you can't resist the impulse to eat.

Angeline gave me a bottle of something that I have to spray it with every hour or so, and some little bottles of a special shampoo she mixed up.

My hair and I will be making some serious plans for our future. I think that things are going to be very different for us now. I wonder if I should name my hair.

## Saturday 14

Dear Dumb Diary,

My hair and I got up a little early today. I slept with it in a protective pillowcase and immediately gave it a big breakfast of shampoo and this spray that it likes so much. While I was brushing it, I looked out my window and thought of all the people with ugly hair. I nearly cried a real tear, except that Angeline said salt water isn't good for my hair so I laughed at them instead.

At breakfast, my mom said she loved my hair, but my dad was all "Why did you do that to yourself?" and "I liked it better before."

Sometimes it's very clear to me that I didn't just come from my dad. I actually *evolved* from him.

It was extra-good that I didn't have school today. That way I could spend some quality time with my quality hair before it has to be exposed to the foulness of the world. I wonder if I can make it a requirement that icky kids aren't allowed to look at it. My uncle *is* the assistant principal. Maybe he can hook me up.

I wonder why Angeline never thought of making that rule before? I guess this is what comes from being smart *and* beautiful.

Isabella called today (like, eleven times) to find out about her puppy, and I had to keep telling her that Angeline said it wasn't ready and she'd just have to be patient. Isabella started yelling that she wanted it before all the cuteness wore off. (Or is that cutenicity?)

I think I hear my hair getting up from its nap, so I gotta go.

# Sunday 15

Dear Dumb Diary,

Sunday is homework day, the day Isabella usually comes over, but I really didn't want to hear her complain about the puppy, so I didn't invite her.

I was kind of surprised when my mom called up to me that "my friend" had arrived to do homework, even though Isabella is not a person that lets a lack of an invitation get in the way of her showing up.

By the age of six she had snuck into at least ten birthday parties of kids she didn't know.

But it wasn't Isabella. It was **Angeline.** And she had her backpack, full of homework.

"Thanks for inviting me over, Jamie," she said. "I do my homework throughout the week so it doesn't all back up on Sunday, but I can double-check my work while you do yours."

I can't tell you how many things were wrong with this:

- Angeline at my house.
- Somebody who does their homework throughout the week.
- Double-checking. (I mean, how do you even *do* that? If you're too dumb to get it right the first time, you're too dumb the second time, too, right?)

And the natural color of her cheeks looks like she's wearing a lot of makeup so she should wear a lot of makeup to cover that up.

I asked Angeline if we had planned this little homework date earlier and it had just slipped my mind.

She said she came over because I had called her house and invited her.

Then I nearly knocked Angeline over as I blew out the door past her.

I ran all the way to Angeline's house, my exquisite hair trailing behind me like ribbons of caramel silk. I know this because every time I passed a parked car I checked out my reflection in the windows. Plus, I pay very close attention to candy commercials that feature caramel.

By the time I got to Angeline's house, Angeline had caught up to me. We were both wheezing and holding our guts and trying to talk in that broken way that you do when you've been running.

"What's. The. Deal. Jamie?" Angeline huffed.

"Check. The. Puppies. That. Wasn't. Me. That. Called," I puffed back.

YOU CAN BE DROPPING DEAD AND STILL BE DROP DEAD BEAUTIFUL

Angeline went inside for a minute, then came back out and sat down on the porch.

"My mom says that a girl was just here claiming to be you, saying that she needed to pick up one of the puppies because Stinker was getting sick from missing his children and would probably die within the hour if he didn't get to see one of them."

"Claiming to be me?"

"My mom says that she either had a really ugly wig or a gopher on her head," Angeline said. "But my mom knows I fixed your hair, so she knew that the girl wasn't you. When she said she knew it wasn't you, the girl just ran away."

I told Angeline that it was Isabella. She hadn't seen me with my gorgeous new hair yet. And it was Isabella who had called, pretending to be me and inviting Angeline over to do homework.

"Really? She sounded exactly like you. But wasn't it kind of dumb to send me to your house?"

"Not if it had worked," I said. If my hair hadn't been different, Isabella would have the puppy, and we would know that she had outsmarted us, which would have made her even happier. Even **wayway** happier. Perfect crime does that for Isabella.

She would have been so WAYWAY that she'd WEE WEE

Angeline said that I should skip the homework and just go home to spend the rest of the day brushing. My hair is yummy, but it is a **lot** of work.

I thought about calling Isabella to accuse her of an attempted pupnapping, but she'd just deny it and then put her fake dad on the phone to say she had been home the whole time.

No, sometimes it's best to just let her crimes go uncaught.

For instance, 301 (and counting) Loud and intensely sour farts.

## Monday 16

Dear Dumb Diary,

It would be hard not to deeply love my hair when you see it. It shines and billows like satin curtains and flows behind me like a big beautiful flag from some exotic country whose entire culture is based on brown hair.

It would be very difficult to trust anybody that didn't love it as deeply as is normal to do.

Hudson Rivers noticed it, and it's obvious that he is completely mesmerized by it.

Margaret noticed it, and was so taken that she briefly stopped eating her pencil to eat out her own heart with envy. (You might recall, Dumb D, that Margaret is such a big-time pencil chewer that her burps smell like a lumberyard.)

Isabella noticed it, and said, "Angeline did this, right? Like, Friday, I'm guessing? It's stunning. Where's my puppy?"

Sorry, I had to stop writing for a minute to spray and brush. This hair of mine is very high-tech.

I told Isabella that the puppy is growing as fast as it can, and that we even stacked some books on Angeline's dog to make the milk come out faster.

We didn't, of course, and I'm not even sure that would work, but by that time Isabella was running her fingers though my hair in such a way that I knew she could jerk it all out of my scalp in one tug if she felt like it.

Isabella thought for a moment.

"Like squeezing a juice box," she said. "Good idea."

And that was that. Isabella seemed satisfied that we are force-milking Angeline's dog. She didn't even seem terribly jealous of my hair, which was a little mean of her, but I know that deep down she probably hates me for it, and that's gratifying.

You're the worst.
Hate is one of the most genuine forms of Admiration!

While Isabella and I were talking, I noticed Hudson Rivers watching. I can only imagine how wrong he must feel for ever thinking Angeline had nicer hair than me. I'm thinking about maybe giving him a wad of it from my brush.

How Hudson Might Enjoy My Hair Wad
GLUE IT TO HIS FACE AS A MANLY BEARD-MOUSTACHE COMBO

HAVE IT MADE INTO A TOOTHBRUSH FOR the MOST GLAMOROUS ORAL HYGIENE EXPERIENCE OF A LIFETIME

STUFF IT INTO HIS SHOES FOR the sensation of running barefoot on my head.

# Tuesday 17

Dear Dumb Diary,

I haven't been doing my fake diary entries! Dumb Diary, how could you let me forget?? I'm going to slam you a bunch of times really hard for a punishment.

Today in Mr. Evans's class he reminded us that we only have three days to complete our fake diary entries. Some people had already turned theirs in early. And he brought up the magazine quizzes again and said that I had suggested such a great idea, that maybe our next assignment could be to write a quiz. This would make me **the mother of an assignment**, which is sickening beyond description, and one of the **worst** things you can be.

I heard about this one girl who was just walking down the street and accidentally blurted out, "Write an essay." Now she's the mother of that assignment and she has to live with the pain and the guilt forever.

Between that and other homework, I was afraid my hair's shimmer was suffering. At lunch,

I asked Hudson if he thought it looked any less shimmery and he said, "What?" I think that probably meant "no," but to be sure I asked about a dozen other people.

It's AMAZING, isn't it?
when you think of how my hair must inspire the nasty, normal-haired people of the world.

Isabella says that I'm fussing over it too much, which made me and my hair feel good because that means she's finally getting in touch with her jealousness of us.

Isabella also had some of her magazine quizzes today and she asked me super-politely if I'd like to do one, but it was in that kind of super-polite way that super-villains talk to superheroes they have chained to a table while they're preparing to blow up the world.

I told her I'd pass, and then she said, OH BY THE WAY, as a comparison, she'd stuck a juice-box straw through a little hole she made in a gallon of milk and stacked a bunch of books on it and it was pretty much empty in about an hour, and isn't Angeline's dog just about squeezed flat by now?

It's very difficult to argue with a good scientist. It's even harder to argue with a good scientist who is eyeing your silky mane in a scary way. I told Isabella that she could come and pick out one of the puppies, rename it, and cuddle on it a little bit, but it still wasn't time to take it home. That seemed to be enough to calm her down. Also, she is very curious to see how flat Angeline's dog is.

HOW ISABELLA IMAGINES ANGELINE'S DEMILKED DOG.

Yikes. It's been a while since I did one of my fake entries. I hope I remember how it goes:

*My Dearest Diary:*

*If there's one thing that my beautifulness teaches us, it is that other people, all over the world, no matter who they are or where they're from, have one important thing in common. They are just not as beautiful.*

*Sincerely,*
*Anonymous but now that you know I'm beautiful, it's probably not too tough to figure out who I am*

PEOPLE OF ALL NATIONS JOIN TOGETHER IN A PERFECT HARMONY OF GROSSNESS.

I have to remember to talk to Angeline about Isabella coming over to pick out a puppy. Obviously, she'll pick out the cutest one and name it Deathbite or Sugarwhatever. Isabella is easy to predict, especially by somebody with magazine-verified smarts.

The Lives of Magazine Quiz Writers
A. I WOULD LIKE PIZZA
B. I WOULD LIKE STEW.
C. I WANT SOME FISH.
D. GIVE ME THAT PIE.
They go to FABULOUS restaurants, but prefer to be given just four choices.

When answering email, they often write upside-down at the bottom of the page.

When choosing an outfit each day, they must remember not to select NONE OF THE ABOVE.

# Wednesday 18

Dear Dumb Diary,

Lunchtime today was a series of conversations in which Isabella just kept trying to change the subject:

**Me:** So have you noticed how beautiful my hair and I look today?

**Isabella:** Yeah. You know what else is beautiful? Puppies.

**Me:** Right. Doesn't their hair look nice when you brush it?

**Isabella:** It does. You sure are smart. I guess you could answer every question in any magazine quiz anywhere.

**Me:** I have a sore on my lip.

**Isabella:** Puppies have sores.

Incredibly, I was actually **GLAD** when Angeline sat down at our table. I wonder if I'm beginning to hate Angeline less. I think my hair hates her hair less. I think my everything-elses still hate her everything-elses. I'm sure her everything-elses feel the same about me and mine.

Angeline asked how our diary things for Evans were going. Isabella said she hates it, like all homework, and it sure would be nice to have a dog to eat her homework once in a while.

I was so desperate to change the subject I actually got into a conversation about homework.

"It's doubly hard for me since I already keep a real diary, and now I have to keep this fake one," I said. Angeline said she was doing exactly the same thing.

Angeline probably writes with A REAL ANGEL FEATHER dipped in FRESH UNICORN SLOBBER for ink.

(UNICORN SLOBBER IS A very pretty pink color)

UNICORN SLOBBER

I remembered one time before, when Angeline had told me she kept a diary. I know what you're thinking, Dumb Diary. You're thinking I have a spectacular memory. And you're right.

But I was surprised to hear that Angeline is smart enough to do exactly what I'm doing. She must have heard me or another genius talking about it and imitated it the way a blond baboon or blond orangutan would.

DUE TO
ITS BLONDENESS,
MONKEY EXPERTS
CONSIDER THE
BABOON THE YUCKIEST.

# Thursday 19

Dear Dumb Diary,

After school, Isabella and I went over to Angeline's house to get her puppy. Isabella was so happy she did that thing where somebody just grabs your hands and shakes shakes shakes them. I think the gesture is universally known as HAPPY INSANE HANDS.

it was irritating, but it made my hair bounce attractively

I'm not sure I've ever seen Isabella so happy. One time a few years ago, this mean old man who lives on our street was yelling at us to get off his lawn. When he turned to go back in the house, he closed the door on his finger and broke it in about a hundred places because old people break easy. Isabella was pretty happy then. She can still sing the song she wrote about it. And I'll bet she still has that T-shirt she made.

But she was even happier about the puppy.

Angeline's dog, Stickybuns, was less nervous now, and the puppies were even more adorable than before. They climbed all over us and licked at us. I tried to remember when Stinker was cute like this and not just mushy and smelly like a dog-shaped peach that has been out on the counter too long.

I **wayway** wish I had a cute dog.

Even at His ABSOLUTE PUPPY-CUTEST, STINKER LOOKED LIKE
A LUMP
THAT ANOTHER DOG HAD REMOVED.

Isabella played with all of the puppies, kind of making them audition for the role of Her Dog. Stinkette was in there, really truly trying her ugly best, but it was pretty clear to everybody that **The Bubblegum Duchess, Prince Fuzzybutt,** and **Dingledongle** were truthfully some of the cutest puppies that were ever born. They were cute enough even to be on a poster with a bowl of spaghetti dumped on their heads, and that type of cute just doesn't come along every day.

Finally, Isabella said she had made her choice. Angeline stood up and stepped on a puppy's head.

Or she *thought* she had. Just like I thought I had. And as Angeline jumped back, she went over — all the way over and hit the ground, hard. She started crying and howling, and her mom came in and said she was afraid that Angeline had broken her ankle.

Isabella and I had to leave without her puppy, which I thought was going to be a huge problem, but Isabella hardly threatened either one of us. I guess she may have felt a little sorry for Angeline, and is kind of okay with waiting a couple more days.

Because my hair is NOW STUNNING, I felt more pity for HER THAN I DID when ONLY Hers was.

# Friday 20

Dear Dumb Diary,

I got called down to the office today. My Aunt Carol works there, you know, with my Uncle Dan, who is the assistant principal, and who, you might recall, happens to be Angeline's uncle.

Aunt Carol said Angeline's mom brought in Angeline's diary assignment because she knows it's due today, and Angeline still can't walk on her messed-up ankle. Angeline wasn't sure if it went to Mr. Evans or to Mrs. Penney, so she asked her mom to make sure I got it.

DIARY
from Angeline's Mom to AUNT CAROL
DIARY
from Aunt CAROL to me, who has the prettiest-drawn hand.

I'm a little worried, because Angeline had to go and make her diary **wayway** thicker than mine. It's almost as thick as my real diary. I wondered if I could go back and add some junk to mine before I turned it in, but there wasn't time.

Angeline's BLUBBERY DIARY ASSIGNMENT
SO SHOW-OFFY she even did it in a REAL DIARY!
MY SLENDER AND TRIM ASSIGNMENT OF REASONABLE LENGTH

I gave my diary to Mr. Evans, along with Angeline's. He scribbled over the names and handed them right back to me.

"Take all the diaries down to Mrs. Penney and she'll tell you what to do," he said in a way that was less **ugly-faced** and **mean-voiced** than usual.

Down in the library, Old Mrs. Penney looked over the diaries.

OLD MRS. PENNEY WEARS THOSE GLASSES ON A CHAIN. WHY??
BAM
Perhaps Librarians get in lots of spirited discussions about books and they don't want to lose their glasses.

"Good. Mr. Evans took the names off." She handed me about a quarter of them. "You type these up, and I'll do the rest," she oldly said, and then added, "I already typed up the ones that were handed in early. And I have some from other classes."

She handed me a stack and put one of the typed ones on top. "Have a look at that one, Jamie. I think you'll find it very interesting." She giggled a little, although I think when old people giggle it's called cackling.

Like when OLD people Dance it's called A SPASM.
AND WHEN They WALK IT'S CALLED STANDING STILL
And when they go to the BATHROOM IT'S CALLED READING FOR 40 MINUTES

## Saturday 21

Dear Dumb Diary,

My hair and I had such wonderful dreams. We were skipping along in a perfect meadow, and my hair was sort of like this beautiful **hair-octopus**, and I would extend a hair-tentacle to gently pet bunnies or puppies or koalas and they would kiss my hair and smile. Also my hair strangled a few of the uglier creatures nobody likes, which might have been kind of mean, but you really must trust the judgment of hair this attractive.

Then my hair reminded me that I had to type up a bunch of diaries, and I woke up.

After about a solid hour of brushing, I began to examine the diaries.

I knew it would be easy to figure out which was which. My brilliant mind could easily unravel the writers' identities, even though only a few were of any interest to me. I found Isabella's right away because I recognized her handwriting. She already tells me everything, so there was no reason to read that one.

Angeline had already told us hers was totally fake, so there was no point in reading that either. I mean, what's it going to say? *Dear Diary, I'm perfect, everybody loves me, but I hate everybody because nobody is as great as me?* Please.

The only diary I really wanted to read was Hudson Rivers's. I quickly flipped through them all, looking for key words. If I saw words like "leotard" or "moisturizer" or "cleanliness," I knew that it wasn't his. These words are unknown to boys' minds until they are afflicted with older age.

On the other hand, words like "video game" or "video games" or "video gamer" are words that often appear in boys' mouths, and are likely to appear in their writing as well.

And then it occurred to me! Old Mrs. Penney told me that one diary in particular would be interesting to me. And she knows all the kids! She knows all about Hudson and me! I quickly found the diary she pointed out. Here's what it said:

**HEY DIARY:**
**I SAW HER AT SCHOOL TODAY AND I THINK HER HAIR LOOKS REAL GOOD. I THINK SHE IS REAL GOOD AND I LIKE HER. THAT IS ALL I HAVE TO SAY TODAY DIARY SO BYE.**

At first, I thought that entry could be about Angeline. Some people might think that she has nice hair. But then I read the rest. Here are a few more entries that I think tell the whole story.

MY HAIR CAN'T REALLY DO THIS YET

HEY AGAIN DIARY:
I THOUGHT ABOUT IT AND NOW I DON'T THINK SHE IS GOOD BECAUSE SHE'S ALWAYS SO CONCERNED ABOUT HER HAIR AND THAT'S PRETTY CONCEITED. OKAY BYE.

HEY DIARY. IT'S ME AGAIN.
NOW THAT I THINK ABOUT IT, I THINK IT'S GROSS AND CRAZY TO BE OBSESSED WITH YOUR LOOKS SO MUCH THAT YOU LET IT CONTROL EVERYTHING YOU DO. I FARTED IN MATH. BYE.

HEY DIARY. I'M WRITING AGAIN.
IT IS A REAL SHAME THAT SOMEBODY SO COOL AND FUNNY REALLY THINKS THAT ALL ANYBODY CARES ABOUT IS LOOKS. PEOPLE CAN'T HELP BUT NOTICE HOW PEOPLE LOOK, BUT THAT'S ONLY A SMALL PART OF WHAT MAKES A PERSON WHO THEY ARE. BYE.

**OKAY DIARY. IF ONLY SHE COULD JUST BE HERSELF AND STOP WORRYING ABOUT HER LOOKS SHE WOULD BE PERFECT. I INVENTED A NEW KIND OF SLOPPY JOE AT LUNCH. IT HAS NO BUN AND IT'S JUST CALLED A SLOPPY. BYE.**

Did you catch it, Dumb Diary? It was that part about "cool and funny." I'm sure this is Hudson's diary, and I'm sure this was about me. Hudson is right. Completely Right. This hair thing isn't me. I'm not the beautiful-hair girl. I'm cool and funny. Oh Hudson, thou art so wise. Wise enough even to be Thou Arted.

Now it's so clear. Angeline gave me this hair to make Hudson reject me. I should have guessed. It's just like her to kill me with beautifulness, her obvious weapon of choice. And now that I think about it, she got me over to her house on the made-up reason of needing help to name the puppies.

Her dog is named STICKYBUNS — only the third or fourth cutest name I've heard of for a dog. She has **no problem** coming up with names. The whole scam was all to get my guard down, to fill my head with puppy fumes, then to spring her trap.

I'm just thankful I found out in time — before I became so gorgeous that there was no turning back.

I called Isabella and told her everything. She said that none of it made any sense, but that I should not bring it up with Angeline until she gets her puppy, and to keep working on the diaries.

MORE OF THE CUTEST NAMES IN THE HISTORY OF DOG NAMES
WEENER SHWEENER

# Sunday 22

Dear Dumb Diary,

Isabella came over today because it's homework day. (I'll bet it's always been like this. I'll bet the pyramids were due on a Monday, but they didn't start making them until Sunday afternoon.)

I stopped brushing and spraying my hair last night, of course. It is in a state of decay, but I am still partially breathtaking. (I'm thinking about having a funeral for the beautiful hair wad I pulled out of my brush.)

Hair today, Gone Tomorrow

In the middle of our homework, **Angeline** called. After what she did. Can you believe the nerve? Here is our conversation:

**Angeline:** Hi, Jamie. How's the diary project coming?

**Me:** (coldly) Just fine. How are the puppies?

**Angeline:** They're great.

**Me:** Wait. I didn't hear what you said.

Isabella lunged at the phone.

**Angeline:** I said they're great. Want me to bring one over for Isabella?

**Me:** I thought your ankle was messed up.

**Angeline:** Oh, yeah. I guess I can't do that. You guys could come over here.

**Me:** I could send Isabella over to pick one.

**Angeline:** No. No. Don't do that. I mean, my ankle hurts again. I have to go. Bye.

It was all I could do to keep myself from calling her a **big fat faker liar**.

It's one of the worst kinds of fat faker liars.

There was no way to finish typing up all the diaries today. Isabella spent too much time on non-homework stuff. And now that I think about it, Isabella wasn't even on my neck about the magazine quiz that I never finished. Mostly all she wanted to do was talk about stuff we had done together, which was weird.

Made snowlady wearing Isabella's Mom's underwear.

Tried to make all the bugs on my street get married.

Hid for 6 hours until her mom calmed down about the snowlady incident.

## Monday 23

Dear Dumb Diary,

I threw away the stuff Angeline gave me for my hair, and it's back to its former mutation. I miss my gorgeous mane, but I had no idea how long people spend on their beautiful hair. Add the makeup and outfits and it's anybody's guess who spends more time on their looks: models or clowns.

When Angeline saw me at school she sucked in a breath, probably because she knew that all of her wicked sorcery on my head had come undone. Her ankle seemed like it was all better and she just stood in front of me, not saying anything, like she was waiting for me to say something. Finally, I couldn't help myself.

"I know what you did."

Angeline looked like she might cry.

"Awful, right?" she said, which of course she is..

"Yes, you are," I said, because she is. (Remember, Diary? I just told you that.)

"But you know that my heart is in the right place," she said.

I must have looked like I didn't know anything about her heart or where she had it, because she narrowed her eyes and said, "Did you finish working on the diaries?"

Something unusual was forming in Angeline's HEAD. Like a thought.

I told her I hadn't and she asked where they were. I told her that Isabella was going to drop them off with Old Mrs. Penney.

Angeline turned around and **RAN** toward the library.

The last time
I saw a BLOND
RUN THIS FAST,
IT WAS A GOLDEN
RETRIEVER AND
THERE WAS A TENNIS
BALL INVOLVED.

By the time I had caught up, Isabella was sitting at a table with the neat stack of diaries in front of her. Angeline was standing there, puffing.

"Are those all the diaries?" Angeline asked.

"All the ones Jamie had." Isabella grinned. "Every single one."

"Including ***Hudson's***," I said meanly, like a mean person pointing out something a meaner person had done.

Isabella laughed a little. "I know which one you're thinking of, Jamie. That wasn't Hudson's," she said.

USUALLY SMILES ARE NICE THINGS.
USUALLY.

I grabbed it out of the pile and shoved it at Angeline. "It is so. Read it, Angeline. I know what you did to me."

Angeline read it and said, "Isabella's right. This isn't Hudson's. It's written too well. Plus, Hudson is pretty much oblivious to you, Jamie. He doesn't notice me anymore, either."

Angeline shuffled through the stack and found a dirty, poorly written diary that looked like it had been dirtily folded and kept in a dirty pocket for a dirty while.

"This is Hudson's. Read it. I'll bet I can already tell you what it says."

I read a couple entries — enough to make things clear to me. The most telling entry said:

dear diary:

I saw a video game in a magazine and I want to get it.

ON TV I saw a car I want someday.

I like pizza and I want to have some for dinner.

Isabella is the coolest girl that ever lived.

Bye.

"Isabella?" I said. "Hudson and **Isabella?**"

"Jamie, you could tell, couldn't you? I mean, anybody could tell," Angeline said.

"Anybody could tell," Isabella echoed. "Not like I care. He's a dope. If you had read my diary, you would have known that."

It was like my brain was playing clips from old tapes. In one, I saw Hudson smiling at Isabella. In another, I heard him asking her to go for tacos after the dance. In another, I saw Stinker choking on a pair of my mom's pantyhose. Guess I had that tape misfiled.

"But, Angeline, you lied about not being able to name the puppies. It was part of your scheme. You came up with the name 'Stickybuns,' only about the third cutest name ever," I said.

"Stickybuns was a ***rescue dog***, Jamie. Remember? She had a name when I got her. You can't change that. It's **Puppylaw**, and everybody knows that."

But **OH–HO**! I found a flaw in Angeline's little alibi.

"Then why did you fix my hair?" I said triumphantly.

"Because I thought you'd like it," Angeline said. Isabella shrugged her shoulders and tilted her head, which is Isabella-language for "and there you have it."

Then Isabella handed Angeline her own diary assignment back.

"Bet you're looking for this," Isabella said.

"Did you read it?" Angeline asked.

"Some of it," Isabella said. "Enough, I think." She started to laugh.

Angeline seemed interested in getting it back
NAB

Old Mrs. Penney finally came over, scooped up all the diaries, and said she'd finish typing the ones that I hadn't.

We all walked out of the library. I'm still not sure exactly what happened. I didn't understand Isabella's exchange with Angeline about Angeline's fake diary, and I was too stunned to quiz them about it.

I don't think anything will ever ever ever ever top *THE ISABELLA AND HUDSON THING*. I'm considering flushing all of this down my brain hole anyway.

## Tuesday 24

Dear Dumb Diary,

I sat with Isabella at lunch today, like always, and I saw Hudson looking over at us, even though now I realize that he's actually looking at Isabella. I should have seen this coming. They have so much in common, like, um, masculinity.

But sort of like how being famous made those ugly boy-girls in the magazine more handsome, seeing Isabella crushed on makes her seem prettier. And since it's Isabella and not Angeline, I really don't mind at all that Hudson isn't focused on me. At all. Even a little. Like a jerk.

Angeline walked by and said hi, but clearly had no intention of slowing down. And then Isabella Spilled It.

"**That was Angeline's REAL diary,**" she said. "You know how both you and Angeline made a fake one just for the assignment? Her mom dropped off the real one by accident. That's why Angeline was in such a panic. She thought you had already read it."

"And you read it??" I asked, hoping that Isabella had violated the **Sacred Secrecy of the Diary**.

"I didn't have time to read all of it. But I read some."

I begged Isabella to tell me what it said, and she threw that dumb **Sacred Secrecy of the Diary** thing in my face.

I explained that privacy and sacredness are really more guidelines than rules. They're really meant to be sacred suggestions.

Then Isabella said, "There's stuff about Angeline you would never have guessed. But I don't want to violate your whole big sacred thing."

Isabella only follows rules when it is WRONG to do so.

"Violate it," I said, loud enough for Bruntford to walk over and tell me to be quiet through that giant hole in the front of her face.

"Violate it," I whispered.

"Okay," Isabella said, and she began to tell me what she read in Angeline's diary. For starters, Angeline didn't hurt her ankle that day with the puppies. She **faked** that. And she learned how to do it by watching Isabella fake injuries. Isabella and I both had to stop and give some respect to the fakery. Isabella especially liked how Angeline bit her lower lip in agony.

"Nice touch," she said. "She fooled me." And I nodded. I think now we know how teachers feel when they see real progress in a student.

"But **why** would she do that?" I asked.

"Because she knew which puppy I was about to choose, and that was the one **she** wanted."

They were all adorable, except Stinkette. What difference could it make?

"Angeline likes us, Jamie," Isabella said. "She thinks of us as friends. But you knew that already, because you know how everybody feels about you, right?"

"Yes," I totally lied. "I totally do."

And then Isabella explained that Angeline wrote about how she was really happy that the puppies connected her to me, and that they connected her to Isabella, too, and how we would all be one big happy family. But she thought that one puppy, in particular, would do that better than the rest. Angeline and Isabella wanted the same puppy.

"She wrote that we'd be like sisters," Isabella said.

The word really hit me. I don't have any siblings. Neither does Angeline. Isabella has brothers, but those are really more like enemies that live at her house.

Sisters. Like my mom and Aunt Carol.

And then Isabella said something I never thought I would ever hear her say.

"I think maybe Angeline isn't a total turd, Jamie. Anybody that fakes an injury like that can't be all bad."

That's high praise from Isabella. That's friend-talk. It's almost exactly what Isabella wrote to me in the first birthday card she ever gave me. I thought that Hudson and Isabella was tough to swallow, but now Angeline and Isabella? **Friends? Sisters?**

I looked out the window to see if it was the end of the world, like if it was raining lizards or a big earthquake was tearing a huge crater in the earth that would swallow all of humanity. Then I wondered for a moment — if that happened, would the news anchors get to report it, or would it be more of a weathergirl thing?

There was one more question I needed answered, and only Old Mrs. Penney could do that. I went to the library and asked her why she told me to look at that one diary in particular.

"I've been here a long time, Jamie," she said.

"Like since right after the earth started cooling," I offered quietly, counting on her old ears not being able to hear it.

"That diary was from another student. One from a long time ago, when I first started here."

"Who?"

She looked at me very seriously and said, **"George Washington."**

And then she started to laugh. I guess maybe she had heard my little joke.

"That diary was your dad's, Jamie. He did the exact same assignment when he was your age. I thought you'd like to read it."

Uck. I can't believe that this assignment actually made me call my dad wise. Further proof that assignments of any kind are bad for people. And to double the uck-factor, he was writing about some girl who was not my mom. (He met my mom in college.)

I told Mrs. Penney that the next assignment will probably be worse and that it's my fault. I told her it was going to be writing a magazine quiz.

"I'm not surprised Mr. Evans is doing that," she said, and my guts tensed up waiting to hear why.

when tense,
guts are even grosser than usual

"Teachers don't make a lot of money, Jamie. Mr. Evans does some freelance writing. He writes a ton of those quizzes for magazines. I'm sure you've done them."

And now the very assignment I gave birth to has turned around and made me refer to Mr. Evans as smart and a Genius and supercool. This has been a long day, Dumb Diary. I have to go to bed. I've said a lot of things I wish I hadn't meant.

TEACHERS
CREATURES OF MYSTERY
They have been spotted wearing normal non-teacher clothes
some of them actually like kids for no good reason.
INCREDIBLY, THEY DO NOT FEEL PAIN OF ANY KIND DURING A HISTORY LESSON!!!

# Wednesday 25

Dear Dumb Diary,

It was a half day at school today. I don't know why. Sometimes teachers say that they use half days to work on grades or something. I think they might just be hosing the coffee odor off each other in the parking lot.

Isabella was sort of smiley all morning, so I kept waiting for something terrible to happen, but it never did.

When I got home, Mom was in a strange mood — sort of angry but also sort of happy. Would you call that **Hangry**? I don't even know where that emotion comes from.

But I had a better idea when Aunt Carol showed up with Angeline, Isabella, and a **basket**.

"We have puppies!" Aunt Carol sang, and Stinker started barking like crazy. Mom tried to look all angry and upset but it is scientifically impossible to look meanly directly at a puppyface.

Stinker was sniffing at all of them and wagging his tail and they were all jumping up on him like he was not ugly or disgusting.

Isabella scooped up The Bubblegum Duchess. "This one is mine," she said. "And I'm not renaming her. Although I'll probably call her Bubs."

Angeline hugged Prince Fuzzybutt. "I'm keeping this one."

Then my mom said in her pretend angry voice, "Go ahead, Jamie. Pick one."

I couldn't believe it. I almost started to cry.

Just Dingledongle and Stinkette were left. The choice seemed obvious. I grabbed Dingledongle and cuddled her close. She was the most adorable puppy I had ever seen.

But Stinkette was rolling around on the ground wrestling with Stinker and the two of them were in some kind of gross ugly love. I handed Dingledongle to Aunt Carol.

"I changed my mind. **I'm keeping Stinkette.**"

Angeline and Isabella smiled. Turns out, Stinkette was the one they both wanted.

Probably
Has
Baby
fleas

They said they thought there was more of a bond between Stinker and Stinkette. They both felt more connected to me and Stinker through her ugliness, I guess. Since they both wanted Stinkette, they decided that, to be fair, neither should get her.

Isabella told me that if I had read her diary, I would have known that already. I think Isabella has been trying to tell me in her diary how she felt all along. She wanted to tell me about Hudson. She wanted to tell me that she felt left out of the whole puppy thing. She wanted me to know that she resented my glamorous hair.

Isabella was worried that she could lose her best friend. But she would never say something drippy like that out loud. Isabella says emotions like that are for grandmas and dance instructors.

I guess she's not comfortable with her sensitive feelings.

"I can fix Stinkette up, you know," Angeline offered.

I said I didn't think that was Stinkette's style. Stinkette wants to be cool and funny.

My mom pressured Aunt Carol into keeping Dingledongle, even though she said my Uncle Dan was going to hit the roof when she got home.

Isabella said her mom was going to do the same thing, and she was not looking forward to the fight.

"Want us to come with you?" Angeline asked. "Moms don't freak out if other kids are there."

Isabella stopped in her tracks and turned to look at Angeline. Angeline was right and Isabella knew it. She was a little shocked that anybody besides me would ever *offer* to help her.

So the three of us went over to Isabella's house and it turns out we were dead wrong. Isabella's mom **DID** freak out.

But evidently, we helped keep the freakiness to a minimum and she didn't say no. Isabella gets to keep Bubs, and now we think that her turtle might even be starting to turn around and is planning to stay home, but it will be weeks before we know for sure.

It was a great day, Dumb Diary, and now me and my ugly ugly dogs need to get our beauty sleep. (Some of us more than others.)

I guess LOVE IS BLIND.
IT DOESN'T SMELL very good either.

# Thursday 26

Dear Dumb Diary,

Remember the old days when I thought I knew everything? I thought I'd never want another dog like Stinker. I thought my dad was dumb, my teacher was uncool, and that nobody stood between me and Hudson except Angeline. I thought Angeline didn't like me, and that Isabella hated Angeline, and that the three of us could never be friends together, much less *sisters.*

Think about it: The nice one is mean to me. The mean one is nice to me. We get jealous of each other, mad at each other, and can't believe how dumb the other ones can be. I'm not sure we're becoming sisters — I think maybe we always have been.

I can't believe that I used to think I knew everything back then. I can't believe how dumb I was. I think I've really realized something.

I realize that it wasn't until exactly THIS moment that I really and truly knew everything — at least everything I want to know.

Thanks for listening, Dumb Diary,

Jamie Kelly

P.S. I thanked my mom again for letting me keep Stinkette and she told me not to thank her — thank Aunt Carol. It was Aunt Carol who pressured my mom into saying okay. Then she said, "Thank your lucky stars you don't have a sister, Jamie. They can get you into more trouble than anybody."

# DEAR DUMB DIARY,

## CAN'T GET ENOUGH OF JAMIE KELLY?

### CHECK OUT HER OTHER DEAR DUMB DIARY BOOKS!

YEAR TWO: #1: School. Hasn't This Gone On Long Enough?

YEAR TWO: #2: The Super-Nice are Super-Annoying

YEAR TWO: #3: Nobody's Perfect. I'm As Close As It Gets.

YEAR TWO: #4: What I Don't Know Might Hurt Me

WWW.SCHOLASTIC.COM/DEARDUMBDIARY

#1: Let's Pretend This Never Happened

#2: My Pants Are Haunted!

#3: Am I the Princess or the Frog?

#4: Never Do Anything, Ever

#5: Can Adults Become Human?

#6: The Problem With Here Is That It's Where I'm From

#7: Never Underestimate Your Dumbness

#8: It's Not My Fault I Know Everything

#9: That's What Friends Aren't For

#10: The Worst Things In Life Are Also Free

#11: Okay, So Maybe I Do Have Superpowers

#12: Me! (Just Like You, Only Better)

## Best Friends for never.

Dear Dumb Diary,

So now I'm friends with Angeline. This is an Automatic Friendship, and I have to just accept it and make the best of things.

See, if I objected, then Aunt Carol might divorce Angeline's uncle, sending both of them tumbling into a deep pit of depression for the rest of their lives, and Angeline could wind up feeling so guilty that she would have to go be locked up in an old dirty insane asylum for years and years, and Stinker's puppies would grow up not knowing both their parents—and I couldn't live with myself for doing something like that to a puppy.